Seeing Things (Full version)

Nathan E

Published by Nathan E, 2024.

This is a work of fiction. Similarities to real people, places, or events are entirely coincidental.

SEEING THINGS (FULL VERSION)

First edition. April 24, 2024.

Copyright © 2024 Nathan E.

ISBN: 979-8224913206

Written by Nathan E.

Also by Nathan E

Grandfather Clock
The Squirrel
The Glitz
Seeing Things
Seeing Things (Full version)

Watch for more at nephriam@yahoo.com.

This story is dedicated to people who believe that there is more fascinating things out there than we could possibly amagine .

Seeing Things
(Full version)
By: Nathan E

It's the middle of winter in Philadelphia. Early snow , a bashful sun , and bitter cold greets anyone who dares to step out into it very harshly . Ignoring that fact, in the center of town an outside burial service has reached its conclusion . Frozen mourners huddle together exchanging their condolences one to another , as if the deceased had been greatly loved , deeply respected , or both .While oddly , one man chooses to stand alone . He makes no effort to comfort , or be comforted by anyone . He quickly breaks away from the pact , moves briskly out of the graveyard , gets into his car and quickly drives away. Moving smoothly through lite traffic, he's able to quickly merge onto the highway, soon exiting onto Interstate Highway 95 South headed back to Florida. Though he tries to ignore what just took place , his mind won't allow him , and it begins to play back all the things that brought him to this moment in time. He was only seven when things started to fall apart with his parents. His mother , Olivia could no longer take the mental beating dished out by this father , Marcus . So off to Florida they went ,never to return . Wich proved to be best , because shortly after , he re-married . He remembered vividly , the yelling , screaming and accusations constantly hurled at his mother like a violent storm . Then like a storm that passes , calmly he would apologize and say that he didn't realize what he was saying or doing. It was like someone else was living inside of him. Though he never hit or abuse her physically , the scars were still there. She died four years before Marcus , never re-marrying and never really getting over him . No , his father was never missed at least not by him . Then his mind switched into all the rumors that were swirling around , that somehow, he really wasn't his son . though his mother got pregnant with him shortly after high school. Knowing full well that he was the only man she had ever been with prior . Then recently , the call , someone from the hospital called to give him the news . His second wife had never spoken to him until she was making the arrangements for the wake. He couldn't even understand why he felt compelled to go in the first place . What he really couldn't understand , was all the people present for the funeral. They had to know who was really going into the ground . How could he have fooled so many , he surmised that people really do have a funny way of seeing things . With that he was able to put it to rest and settle his mind . With not all that much to keep himself alert, he decides to make a call, on the other end a woman's voice answers.

Voice) " OH hey babe, I was just about to call you, you little mind reader, so ...how did it go?

Man) " OH it was alright "

Voice) " Are you O.K. ? "

Man) " Yeah, yeah I'm alright . I hardly knew him anyway, you know.

Voice) " Yeah, I know , but he was still your father. "

Man) " Yeah, some people say that. "

Voice) (lightly scolding) " Ronnie ...so how are the roads?

Ronnie) " Amazingly clear right now, that's why I wanted to get outta there. "

Voice) " Yeah , O.K. ... are you going to push through? "

Ronnie) " OH yeah, I'm just stopping for gas , food and little pee breaks along the way. (She laughs)

(About a mile up ahead there's a curvature in the road and Ronnie clearly sees a driver out of control.)

Ronnie) " What's he doing? "

Voice) " Ah what, what's who doing? "

Ronnie) " There's a car coming my way that's all over the road."

Voice) (nervous) " Is there any way to go around him ? "

Ronnie) " It's a two-lane highway babe, ... I'll just slow up a bit and punch it when he gets close.

Voice) (really nervous now) " Ronnie , just stop the car and let him go around you. "

Ronnie) " I can't pull over hun , snowbanks on every side . I'll be alright. "

Voice) " Ronnie don't you get off this phone , you hear me? What highway are you on? "

Ronnie) " 95 South , its O.K. honey ,I got this , OH SHIT !!! (She hears tires screeching , then eerie silence)

Voice) (shouting) " RONNIE ! RONNIE ! Ronnie pick up baby (starts to cry and talk at the same time.) " Ronnie pick up , please baby please. "

Ronnie) " He ran off the road and hit a tree just ahead of me a little bit. I'm going to see if he's alright. "

Voice) " Ronnie no ! Ronnie just call somebody, that's what they do , Ronnie are you listening?

(He runs ahead to the crashed vehicle. When he gets there, he sees a lone driver trapped inside. The car is totaled from the impact. But the driver is still coherent , but bleeding from a head wound . Also his body seems to be pinned. As Ronnie tugs on the door it's obvious that the door is jammed . But the driver has managed to roll the window down. Seeing this Ronnie reach's in with both hands attempting to pull the driver out, but to no avail. With the man obviously in a lot of pain , he knows he has to be careful in his next attempt. As he frantically search's about in and around the car for his next course of action, strangely the man summons him with a hand gesture over to him. Once he reach's him, the man grabs his head with both hands and stares into his eyes and says)

Injured man) " Thank God "

(There's a blinding flash of brilliant white light with an explosion, and Ronnie is thrown ten feet through the air onto a nearby snow embankment. The car explodes into a fireball. Pulling back slowly from the scene , we see the car engulfed in flames , then Ronnie unconscious on the snowbank , then back to his car where we can make out the sound of Ronnie's girlfriend talking to someone.)

Voice) " Yes, my name is Kathryn Slater , I was talking to my fiancé and believe he's been in a terrible accident … yes sir… he was on his way back from Philadelphia … about 30 minutes … yes sir that would be…hold on I wrote it down somewhere , yes sir , that would be 95 South headed back to Florida … me? … about 10 to 15 minutes ago now , please hurry !"

(With that we go beyond the car to a snow embankment and dark trees, that all fade to a whiter than white background that re-focuses to a hospital sheet , scrolling up we see Ronnie in bed holding Kathryn's hand with a detective nearby , complete with note pad talking to them.)

Detective) " Between both of your statements we have everything we need . Poor fella must have hit an ice slick in the road and lost control , it happens. The force of the impact with him hitting the tree caused the gas tank to explode , nothing you could have done. If you were any closer to it when it blew , you might not be here talking to me now. Your fiancé's quick thinking saved you more than you know. Giving us the State Road , approximate time you left the funeral and the time you called her , we were able to triangulate your cell phone's signal to assist in identifying your location. Putting all that together we were able to find you in 30 minutes , in the area you were in , it could have been a lot worst.

Ronnie) (squeezing her hand and moving it from side to side) " Oh yes , believe me I know how special she is . "

Detective) " Well here's my card if you remember anything else , or wanted to send me an invitation to the wedding. " (They all share a laugh and the detective leaves. Just as he does , a nurse comes in with a wheel chair to discharge him.)

(A little later , while in the car on the way to back to Kathryn's hotel room Ronnie seems puzzled)

Ronnie) " Kat ? "

Kat) " Yes Ronnie "

Ronnie) " What did I tell the police ? "

Kat) " What ? "

Ronnie) " What did I tell the police ? "

Kat) (nervously laughing a bit) " What do you mean, what did you tell them ? "

Ronnie) " I don't think I told them everything. "

Kat) " Everything like what ? "

Ronnie) " What the detective said about the guy hitting an ice slick , the road was fine , I was standing on it myself , and the car immediately catching fire, Kat , I spoke with the guy , I tried to pull him out! "

Kat) (looking confused) " I heard the crash babe , I heard the explosion , then nothing . " (tears start to fall)

Ronnie) " I'm sorry dear , I didn't mean to bring it up . Let's just check out and get home huh? "

Kat) (wiping her tears) " Yes , let's get you home , we've had enough of Phili ."

Ronnie) (smiling at her) " Yeah ! Yeah, let's get out of Phili ! " (she smiles)

(They arrive back to the hotel and go up to the room . As they begin to pack, she suddenly stops and sits on the bed , and looking at him says)

Kat) " You know Ronnie , you've just had a major trauma , and have been in the hospital for two days. Getting back on the road right this minute , might not be the best idea. " (smiling playfully)

Ronnie) (catching the hint) " You know , you could be right . Sleeping one night in a real bed , undisturbed , might be just what I need. "

(Seeing his agreeing smile, she walks over to him and puts both arms around his neck, they kiss. Moments later there is a do not disturb sign placed on the door. Later , deep into the night while they sleep, the entire scene of what happened replays in his mind . Along with the viewing came automatic questions . Why was he swerving back and forth across the road ? Why did he just run straight into a tree. Who was he , the detective asked us a lot of questions but didn't tell us a whole lot .As he gets to the part of when his face was held, and the blinding light , he shoots straight up in bed greatly disturbed. He could feel it , something shooting straight into his brain , and surging in him as he flew through the air. Looking at Kathryn and seeing how happy she appeared, calms him and he decides to keep the event to himself. While he lays there contemplating what to do, and what does this whole thing mean , he falls back to sleep. Morning comes , they playfully interact , then go to a restaurant for breakfast . In the middle of it Kathryn excuse's herself, and heads to the lady's room. While she's away, still eating, he casually views other patrons in the restaurant . As he does, he sees a flash of brilliant white light that makes him grunt in pain for a second or two. With sight restored , he takes a quick pan around the room to make sure he didn't embarrass himself. Luckily , no one noticed . As he re-settles himself , the strangest thing happens. He notice's a woman passing by his table , as she passes , still viewing her from a side angle , he notices that he is seeing everything she's looking at directly ahead of her. Puzzled , he chuckles to himself not paying it too much attention. Then a man across from him gets up and turns toward the rear of the building , looking at the man , again from a side angle , he is able to see what the man is seeing straight ahead of himself , a restroom sign. A bit more disturbed this time he quickly looks down at the table , disbelieving in what he's witnessing . Looking up again from where he's presently seated , he can't see the restroom sign. Bothered by all this , he gets up and goes over to where the man was seated , looking forward now he clearly sees the sign , thinking to himself, "That's impossible " Just then Kathryn comes out.)

Kat) " OH you have to go too ? "

Ronnie) " Ah yes, if you're on the road, drop your pee or sorry you'll be. (She laughs)

Kat) " I didn't know you were a bathroom poet. "

Ronnie) " A man of many parts dear, many parts . "

Kat) " And one of those parts needs attention right now " (Looking down at his crotch, they both laugh and he goes inside.)

(Not really knowing what to think at this point, he looks in the mirror , and smirks to himself. Then throws some cold water on his face , and speaks to himself in a low tone . " C'mon man get it together , you're alright . The sun is shining , the birds are singing , and your beautiful girl is waiting . He dry's the water off his face , resets himself ,and leaves the restroom. As he returns to the table, she's finishing her drink as he sits down.

Kat) " Everything come out alright ?" (Catching him by surprise)

Ronnie) " OH you got jokes ? (Motioning to the food) " you finished ? "

Kat) " yeah , let's go "

(She asks for the check , the waitress comes over , does her job and brings back her card. With the bill taken care of , she plops down the standard tip and they prepare to leave. Just as they stand up to do so , a woman not paying attention passes close to them causing them to hesitate, letting her by first. Noticing, Ronnie views her from a side angle , and it happens again. He sees everything that the woman is seeing straight ahead. Entranced by this, with his head still turned sideways , he's seeing outside the restaurant , and the car she's getting into. By now Kathryn is noticing him .)

Kat) " She was nice looking but , not that nice . "

Ronnie) (puzzled) " Huh ?... Who ? "

Kat) " The woman that has you in such a trance . "

Ronnie) (still trying to come back to himself) " OH yeah her , yeah, she was alright. "

(They get in the car and drive off. With Kathryn driving he has nothing to do but picture watch out of his window. Seeing open country has a calming effect on him and he starts to relax. She peeps at him and smiles.)

Kat) " So are you going to tell me ?"

Ronnie) (confused) " tell you what ? "

Kat) " What you saw in the restaurant ?

Ronnie) " OH that woman didn't mean anything to me. "

Kat) " I know that , if she did you would have been trying to get that last peek in , but you didn't. So don't make me beg."

Ronnie) (With arms partially up to help with the illustration) " That woman "

Kat) " So you did get that last peek ."

Ronnie) " No , that woman , ... I could see what she was seeing . "

Kat) " What ? ...you mean you knew what she was thinking ? "

Ronnie) " No , ...I ... it happened two other times."

Kat) " Before today ? "

Ronnie) " No , two other times at the restaurant . Once , with a man and once with another woman. I... I could see what they were seeing. "

Kat) (trying to understand) " You could see what they were seeing ? What kind of car was she driving ?

Ronnie) " A blue Honda , license plate EGF 7609 "

Kat) " and the man ? "

Ronnie) " Broke it off when he opened the bathroom door. "

Kat) " Can you see me ? "

Ronnie) '" No "

Kat) " Why ? "

Ronnie) " I don't know , I don't know about any of this. "

Kat) (thinking out loud) " Maybe you've got some kind of crazy concussion or something, you were thrown what, about twelve feet.

Ronnie) " Ten feet , yeah that could be possible but ... "

Kat) " But what ? "

Ronnie) " They worked me up for everything before I left the hospital. "

Kat) " You're right , you want to go back and have them take another look ? "

Ronnie) " No , whatever this is , it will pass, let's just get home. "

Kat) (concerned) " you're alright though ? No headaches , no nausea, no pain ? "

Ronnie) " No , I'm fine. "

(They drive in silence a little further . After a bout of wrestling with himself he starts to explain)

Ronnie) " Kat I need you to listen to me, O.K. ?"

Kat) (confused) " O.K. ? "

Ronnie) " Something happened to me that night. "

Kat) " of course it did dear, you had a terrible accident. "

Ronnie) " No , that's not all of it ... I saw that he'd crossed over the road one last time and ran right into the tree , I mean ..., almost like it was on purpose. If you remember, I told you that before I stopped the car. "

Kat) " Yeah, I do remember you saying that. So why didn't I remember that when detective Monroe asked me ? "

Ronnie) " You were scared for me , somehow you knew it wasn't over . " (She stares ahead mentally putting things together.) " I came back to the car, told you what happened , and what I was going to do . I could hear you calling me but, I don't know, I had to do something . So I ran over to him , he was hurt pretty bad. I tried to pull him out but he was stuck. I was running around the car trying to find something to pry the door open ...why didn't I remember this before ? He was watching a video or something , I saw some people on it doing something, must have been important to him , it was the last thing he was watching. Strangest thing though, it was still running even after he hit the tree. But the part that really got me the most , is when he summoned me back to where he was, he grabbed my face with both hands , looked into my eyes and said "Thank God " , there was a bright light , like in the restaurant , then the explosion. But not the car, ... him. That's what threw me 10 feet away , then the car exploded. I remember that because I could feel the heat from it just before I was unconscious, He gave me something.

Kat) " Gave you what ? "

Ronnie) " Some kind of gift , that lets me see what other people are seeing. I see things through their eye's " (nervously laughs)

(The incredible number of new revelations given to her, makes her pull the car to the side of the road.)

Kat) " Ronnie, you're scaring me, not you but, this thing ...I mean what are we supposed to do with that ? Seeing what other people see ... how long does it last ? "

Ronnie) " I don't know , a few minutes maybe, or I could just keep looking , I don't know ? "

Kat) " Well, let's try it out. You just look at somebody and this thing kicks in, right ?

Ronnie) " Yes "

Kat) " Alright , we'll let you rest until we get back , then we'll go to a mall or something and see if you still have this thing or not.

Ronnie) " Sounds like a plan ... I'm glad I told you; it makes it easier to carry rather than going through this alone.

Kat) " That's what I'm here for, that and you're bank account of course. " (they both laugh)

(Agreeing with Kathryn about his current role , he nods and window gaze the rest of the trip until they reach their destination. Back in Florida now , they go to a nearby mall .)

Kat) " O.K. , let's eat first. You put your shades on and try not to focus on anyone , O.K. ? "

Ronnie) " Almost sounds like you've done this kind of thing before. " (as he dons the shades)

(They have a nice quiet lunch at one of the bodega's and after a bit , it's time to test her theory.)

Kat) (whispering) " Does it work with the shades on or off ? "

Ronnie) " I don't know , I've never done this before ... with the shades I mean. "

Kat) " Well try it " (still whispering)

Ronnie) (With shades on he picks a subject. A young teenage boy walking alone.) " Nothing "

Kat) (still whispering) " Are you sure ? "

Ronnie) (Looking at her mildly frustrated) " Of course, I'm sure . "

Kat) " Pick someone else , that girl over there. "

Ronnie) " Still nothing "

Kat) " Maybe it's gone, O.K. take the shades off , and pick somebody. "

(Looking around briefly , he picks out one of a trio of teen boys walking past.)

Kat) " Well ? "

Ronnie) " Got um " (He gets up and follows them from a distance Kathryn quickly joins him. Soon he begins to laugh .)

Kat) " What ? ...What's so funny ? "

Ronnie) " He's looking at boobs , all sorts of boobs, even the ones on the mannequin . "

Kat) " Of course he is , he's a teenage boy , I'm still not sold. What about that old couple over there ? " (He looks in their direction.)

Ronnie) (smiling) " He just keeps looking at different parts of her . Her hair, her eyes , her mouth as she talks to him. "

Kat) " That's sweet , see how long it last , look away. (He does as instructed after a few minutes it fades.)

Ronnie) " It's gone " (Kathryn looks frustrated with herself)

Kat) " Urgh ! " (Ronnie notices)

Ronnie) " What ? "

Kat) " I didn't time it . "

Ronnie) " It's O.K. I'll just pick someone else. " (She looks lovingly at him and grabs his arm and pulls close to him. He selects someone else) " Got him "

Kat) " Who ? "

Ronnie) " Middle age man over there. (Nodding in a direction)

(They sit down on a nearby bench viewing the man.)

Kat) " What's he looking at ? "

Ronnie) " Everything , and everyone. No wait , the girl across from him in " Donny's " , he's watching her every move. "

Kat) " Like a stalker or something ? "

Ronnie) " No , like someone he likes very much. He smiles at her interactions with customers , the way she strokes her hair, the way she moves, everything about her. "

Kat) " OH my God , he's in love with her ! "

Ronnie) " Problem , he's twice her age. "

Kat) " Knew he was a stalker. " (They exchange a snicker) " O.K. one more , then let's go. "

Ronnie) " O.K. , twenty something on the right . "

Kat) " Yeah I see him "

(Just then Ronnie jumps up and starts running in the man's direction . Confused, Kathryn not really sure of what is going on , just stands and watches. Thirty seconds away , a woman is coming from the opposite direction with a shoulder bag . The watching man leaps out and rips the bag from her shoulder , before he makes a step , Ronnie plows into him. As they wrestle around on the floor, a crowd quickly forms . With her view obscured , Kathryn race's over . In all the commotion security was alerted and quickly reach's the scene the same time Kathryn does. Arriving at the scene , she sees the woman half bent over sobbing , with her clothes in slight disarray, with must hair. Do -gooders in the crowd are holding both Ronnie and the purse snatcher . As security break's the whole thing up.)

Security 1) " Everybody please stand back and let us handle this please. "

Security 2) (Looking at the victim) " You alright mam ? " (With a hand gesture she answers in the affirmative . With two other guards holding each man , the obvious question is asked.)

Security 1) " Anybody see what happened here ? "

Female Customer) (Pointing at the purse snatcher) " This man pushed this woman down and stole her purse. "

Male Customer) " These two guys started fighting over this woman's purse."

Young Couple) (male speaking first) " This dude jumped on this dude and they started tussling ."(female counterpart speaks) " They almost push her down fighting over her purse, I guess both of them wanted it."

Security 1) " Alright that's enough , " (Looking at the two men) " You two are coming with me. " (From the crowd Kathryn speaks out.)

Kat) " Wait a minute ! " (Pointing in the direction of Ronnie) " This man is my boyfriend , and he saw what this man was about to do, ran over here and saved this woman. "

Security 1) (Looking at the victim) " Is that correct mam ?"

Woman) " It all happened so fast , somebody jerked my arm and pushed me , then I saw the two of them rolling around ."

Security 1) " So you don't know who did what , is that right ? "

Woman) " Yes , ... yes that's right ."

Security 1) " Bring um wit me , I'm sorry mam but you have to come too . " (Looking at the victim)

Woman) " I just want to go home ."

Security 1) " Yes mam , but you've been the victim of a crime, and we have to follow procedure, O.K. ? We'll get you outta here as soon as we can, alright ? "

Woman) " Alright "

Kat) " I'm coming too , I'm his witness ." (Security guards look one to another , then agrees.)

(They all go to an office off the main floor with a table and some chairs , a computerized replay system set up on a short wall , and what appears to be a monitor. With everyone inside the lead security agent , calls over one of the other guards close to him and say's in a low voice, " Get 22 " the agent nods and leaves . Everyone sits in silence for a few minutes , then the guard returns with tape in hand.)

Security 1) (Walking over to the replay system) " Before I put this in , is there anything anybody wants to say , because once I do that's it. "

Purse Snatcher) " This dude turned on me man , he set all this up . Told me he was try'n ta get back at his ole lady " (Looking in the direction of Kat) " I doe know who she is , might be his new lady . "

(Security Officer 1 , turns and looks at Ronnie)

Security 1) " Anything to say ? "

Ronnie) " Play the tape "

(He puts the tape in , though the angle is not the best , it does show the man leaning on the wall waiting. He stops the tape and looks at all the surroundings , then starts it again , only to pause it a few seconds later when the victim comes into view. The earlier 30 second delay from reaching the scene saves Ronnie , as the tape is played further it shows the man clearly snatching the purse and Ronnie plowing into him directly after. Upon seeing this the victim reach's over and touch's his arm and quietly says "Thank you " . The lead Security guard looks at one of the other guards and simply says " call um " , with that the purse snatcher gets agitated)

Purse Snatcher) " Call um fa who ? I told y'all man , this dude set the whole thing up ! " (With that he starts to stand up , the other security guards rush over and constrain him , and put a zip tie on his hands. Knowing what's next he begins to struggle , but to no avail, three to one odds are too much to overcome , they quickly remove him .)

Security 1) " I've been doing this for a long time and I knew we had our man when we brought all of you in here, but procedures right ? "

Ronnie) " Procedures right , yeah man I get it , so what's next ? "

Security 1) " Just some statements and forms to fill out , then you can go . One question though , how did you know what he was going to do ? "

Ronnie) " I grew up in Miami , saw a lot of things . "

Security 1) " Miami huh , maybe you ought to come and work for me , it would make my days easier . (They share a slight grin.)

(Shortly after , they finish the paperwork and the appreciative victim thanks him again , followed by a hug. Kathryn notices but doesn't say anything. She simply smiles and wishes her well. With all parties finished now, the victim , under guard, is escorted to her vehicle. Just as Ronnie and Kathryn are about to leave , the lead Security guard has one more comment .)

Security 1) " She's scared right now , but when she tells this story to her lawyer , we'll probably will be getting sued. You're not going to sue us as too, are you ?"

Ronnie) " No , I like this Mall , I want to keep it just the way it is , owning it would be too much of a hassle . " (They share a laugh , shake hands , and leave.)

(They continue on without further incident and reach home. After a lite dinner they go to bed. Again in the middle of the night he re-lives the accident scene as if trying to learn something . Morning comes and they start their morning routine of a lite breakfast and scanning through the mail.

Ronnie) " Hey hon ? "

Kat) " yes baby "

Ronnie) " There's a Carnival in town. I haven't been to one of those in ages , let's go tonight .

Kat) " OH babe , you forgot ? "

Ronnie) " Forgot what ? "

Kat) " OH you did, ... with the accident and all , yeah, I can see that . My cousin 's recital. "

Ronnie) " OH yeah that's right , you've been talking about it for weeks. Yeah, we can't miss that. "

Kat) (thinking) ...you can

Ronnie) " What do you mean ? "

Kat) " She barely knows you , so low expectations , I on the other hand , have known her all her life. She might get mildly miffed if you don't come, but I would have to leave the state. So , I'll go to the recital , we'll do the girly thing afterwards , while you go to the Carnival and be a kid again ,how does that sound? "

Ronnie) " Sounds great ! " (Walks over and gives her a kiss) " Thanks hon . "

Kat) " You bet ... one thing though "

Ronnie) " What ? "

Kat) " Do not return home unless you've bought me a candy apple."

Ronnie) " I promise "

(They kiss again and separate for their day at work. With all the busy demands of work and trying to get back into the swing of things, he doesn't experiment any further with his new found talent , and barely even thinks about it. Now with work being done for the day , his attention switches to the Carnival. He feels very fortunate to have casual dress day at work, making it unnecessary for him to go home and change. With the evening shadows coming in a whole lot sooner because of fall. He only has about an hour and a half to kill before he gets the look he wants, with all the magic of the Carnival atmosphere. He decides to give Kathryn a call , and they share their itineraries for the evening . After a quick meal at one of his favorite spots , it's finally time to be a kid again. He arrives to the atmosphere he wanted , the smell of fresh popcorn , cotton candy , corn dogs and a beautiful crisp night with almost no wind . Just dark enough to appreciate all the colored lights and festive sites. After going around to some of his favorite spots, and tasting the different foods he remembered as a child , his mind slips slowly back onto his new found gift. He decides to take it on another test drive , to get better insight into its capabilities . He perches on one of the stools of a game that had not opened yet , and starts to check out the crowd. Thinking to himself.)

Ronnie) " Woman , at 3 o'clock ...watching her children on the merry-go-round , good. Man at 10 o'clock , eyeballing the pretty girls passing left and right , got it. Woman staring at Ferris Wheel , ...not really sure what she's focusing on ... wait , two mid-teens , got to be her kids. O.K. , now let's see how long I can keep it going. Woman right in front of me with her back turned , should be a good challenge , never viewed from behind. "

(As he tries to use his gift on her, a funny thing happens, he sees himself sitting on the stool. Undaunted , he tries again ... same result. Then the woman turns around , looking right at him. She strangely smiles , and starts to come over. Somewhat rattled by this he's not really sure of what to do. Conflicted , he tries to see what she's looking at one more time , and one more time he sees himself sitting on the stool. Not really knowing what to do at this point , and feeling somewhat afraid, he gets up to leave , when she says the strangest thing.)

Lady) " Doesn't work on me. "

(Feeling trapped and confused , but strangely curious , he allows her to reach him .)

Ronnie) " Why would you say that ? "

Lady) " You were trying to see me , but you couldn't . " (She sits next to him) " You're a seer. "

Ronnie) " I'm a ... excuse me , I'm a what ? "

Lady) " A seer , you see what other people are watching , correct ? "

Ronnie) " How do you know that ? "

Lady) " Because , I'm a seer too. We can see other people , but we cannot see each other. When we try , all we see is ourselves , that's how I knew what you were ."

Ronnie) " But you're back was turned . "

Lady) " Yes , so when you tried to see me , it made me see myself . That's how I knew there was another seer around. Instead of seeing other people , I kept seeing myself . When I turned around, I saw it was you. "

Ronnie) " But how ? ... I mean do "

Lady) " Hello my name is Sophie Monet " (Though still very much confused , he extends his hand and shake's hers.) " Pleased to meet you , and yes , there are more like us out there. I received mine from a dying Aunt at the age of twelve in France . Everyone always knew she was a little off , but I don't think anyone knew it was something like this . Since they couldn't figure it out, they just said that she was eccentric and left it that way. I was always her favorite for some strange reason . That fact was not lost on the rest of the family , so to keep her mind off me , they dominated her time making sure she saw only them. But she in turn , would always schedule a sort of playtime for us both. Finally, with her health failing and her wealth increasing , and further knowing she could not trust them to do what was right, she changed her will and left me everything , including this. "

Ronnie) " How did she do it ? "

Sophie) " The gift you mean ? " (He nods in agreement) " She held me by the face , and looked into my eyes ." (He gasp's) " I take it you got yours the same way . "

Ronnie) " Yes " (somberly) " But what are we supposed to do with it ? "

Sophie) " I struggled with that question for quite a while , then on my 17th birthday , I just decided to enjoy it . Seeing through other people's eyes can be quite entertaining and exhilarating if you know how to use this properly . I've been everywhere and nowhere all at the same time . I could tell you more , but you wouldn't understand what I am talking about at this point in your journey also, I don't what to dampen any curiosity you might have for your own exploration . So I'll tell you a little bit more about me. I find myself frequenting the states more and more these days and not really understanding why . I do remember my loving Aunt talking about the America's , and how much she enjoyed them when she was a girl , but I never thought I'd be fulfilling her childhood dreams into my adulthood . I suppose she has a hold on me still , because I use a modest amount of my wealth for the good of mankind in memory of my beloved Aunt , all else I use for my own enjoyment. " (Tapping him on the leg as she rises to leave.) " You can do a lot more with this than just following people around . "

Ronnie) " Like what ? "

Sophie) " OH you'll figure it out , I'm sure of it. Now that I know you , I'll be checking you out. "

Ronnie) " How ? "

Sophie) " The gift , it works like a tracker , once you meet another seer , you always know where they are and vice-a-versa. I could track 6 , you make 7 , we're scattered everywhere.

Ronnie) " Could you stay for a while longer , I have so many questions about this whole thing. "

Sophie) " I'm sorry my darling boy , but I'm a wealthy woman with many things to see and do while I'm here . Strangely , you've become a part of all that now , with our fateful meeting here tonight . I will tell you this though , seers are chosen for the good they possess inside of them , so you never have to fear them , but there are others ...I'm sure we'll meet again , Mr. ? "

Ronnie) " OH , yes, I'm sorry , Ronald Dobbs, but they call me Ronnie , excuse me , you said others ? "

Sophie) " Yes my darling boy , but we usually refer to them as " the others " and they are not very pleasant. But that's a story for another time " (speaking to him as she starts to walk away) " Enjoy your Carnival Ronnie , and rest you're mind , we'll meet again soon. "

Ronnie) " Soon ? "

Sophie) (Raising her voice slightly) " Sooner than you think. "

(His head begins to spin from all the things that has happened to him in such a short period of time. Stunned , he sits there letting things process . Just as he begins, the carnival game where he's seated begins to open .)

Carnie) " We'll be open in a few minutes' sir , you're welcome to stick around .

Ronnie) " No... no thanks , I think I'll be playing a different game now ."

(With that he rises and leaves , leaving the carnie more than a bit confused. Walking around in a daze he almost leaves before he remembers his promise to Kathryn. Stopping by one of the booths he purchase's the biggest candy apple they have , just as he does a strange smile brightens his face . Somewhat floating now , he leaves the Carnival and returns home . With childlike enthusiasm he enters their home. Kathryn , upon seeing his mood misinterprets the cause.)

Kat) (Looking at the huge candy apple in his hand) " OH babe , you remembered " (Takes the candy apple and gives him a big kiss.)

Ronnie) " Yes love , the biggest one in the place. But that's not why I'm smiling. "

Kat) " No , then what ? "

Ronnie) " I met a woman tonight ! " (She raise's the candy apple as if she's ready to throw it . Quickly realizing his mistake he rephrases) " No , ... I met someone like me . "

Kat) " You're about to eat this Ronald and I don't mean in a good way ! "

Ronnie) " No Kat stop, another seer ! "

Kat) (gasp) " Another ? ... "

Ronnie) " Seer, she was at the Carnival , I was testing my talent on different people and I met her. "

Kat) " How ? "

Ronnie) (excited) " yeah , right so, I was seeing her from behind and she started talking to me and "

Kat) " Ronnie calm down , I know you couldn't possibly be telling it right. "

Ronnie) (takes a breath) " O.K. , her name is Sophie something from France , when I tried to see her, I couldn't , I kept seeing myself , and she kept seeing herself , so that's how she knew that I was a seer .

Kat) (stunned and confused) " I don't know what you are talking about , and what does France have to do with it ?

(He takes her by the hand and leads her to the couch. Then taking both hands in his , he slowly starts to explain everything that happened and what it means. She gets the meaning of the slower version , they embrace , kiss and he ask about her evening at the recital. They laugh about different points in their evenings , then settle into bed. The new day comes, and they go about their usual routines . At different times of his day, Ronnie tries out his new talent with nothing too earth shaking to report. Then one day while sitting at his desk he decides to view a co-worker named Oscar , from his viewing it appears that Oscar has a little more than a schoolboy crush on Amy , who works right across from him . With the two of them being as young as they are , and Oscar being way too shy to strike up a conversation with her . Ronnie decides to put his new found talent to good use . Going back in and viewing him again he sees Oscar constant gazing at the snack machine down the hall , then quickly glancing at Amy's desk . He peeks at her desk several times undetected until he finally sees the chips she likes . In the mist of viewing him , he gets up and goes in the direction of the machine , looking right at it , but strangely pretends that he's not . He does silly things while standing there . Like pretending to read the assignment board , re-tying a shoe that's already tied , to straightening his clothes , all in the quest to see if Amy 's favorite chips are there . Once he's able to get a good undetected look , much to his dismay, they are not. Dejected , he slowly goes back to his desk . Knowing this could crush the poor kid's confidence , Ronnie decides to take matters into his own hands . He stops work and leaves the job goes around the corner , and buys a large bag of Amy's favorite chips , returns to work and plops them down on the kid's desk , and speaking in a low voice say's)

Ronnie) " Hey Oscar , say listen , Kat's crazy over these things , they had a two for at the store , but she'll never eat that much . I don't care for um myself , so I figured maybe you knew somebody that does . "

Oscar) (Seeing the large bag makes his face light up like a Christmas tree) " OH thanks so much Mr. Dobbs , I don't like them all that much either , but I think I know someone that does , thanks again Mr. Dobbs , thanks again ! "

(And with that the deed was done , Amy and Oscar started to be the new talk around the water cooler. Seeing how good it felt to use the gift in a positive way gave Ronnie a new sense of purpose. A couple of days later after playing cupid on the job , he was on his way home , but had to pick up a couple of things from the store . After pulling into the parking lot not really thinking about anything at all , just as he's about to get out of the car , an older woman catches his eye . The thing that did it was the way she kept hesitating not far from the door . So , he sat back down , closed his door and decided to view her . From his viewing of her , he noticed she kept looking in her purse , then she would pause , look up at the sky , then look at the ground . Oddly , when he looked inside the purse with her , there was nothing out of the ordinary . Just some keys , a few folded dollars , a compact , some tissue and a few more odds and ends . But nothing to explain her odd behavior. It took him a few minutes to figure it out. Then smiling he got out of the car and headed her way . However , just as he was nearing her , she went inside . Undaunted , he followed her in . Maneuvering out of her eyesight he follows her around the store . She puts very selective things in her basket , then stops looks at them and puts something back . This strange ritual continues for two more aisles , then he makes his move . Coming up close behind her he softly says)

Ronnie) " Excuse me mam , but I think you dropped this . "

(She turns to see a $50 dollar bill in his hand , lightly shaking as she takes the bill from his hand , tears of joy fall immediately from her eyes . Without saying another word he passes by her and makes his way out of the store forgetting all about what he came for in the first place . Smiling to himself on the way home , suddenly it was clear , this is how he'd use the gift given him , he would use it to help all those who couldn't help themselves , and do it without any fanfare , silently . A few days later while at the gym , a big commotion started about someone stealing a wallet from a locker . Management quickly locked all exiting doors and asked everyone to voluntarily take all contents out of their bags and place them on the gym's floor so they wouldn't have to call the police . Oddly , everyone agreed . While taking the things out of his bag , he begins to read the room . The two younger guys had no problem at all , and continued their casual conversation about things that nothing to do with what was going on . A shapely female seemed more disturbed by this and called over one of the female staff members to view her bag so she wouldn't have to put everything out on the floor . Several other people with all sort of body types showed no problem at all to putting everything down on the floor . But there was one guy , a very talkative overly friendly sort that begged to be viewed . After starting the session on him , he believes that he might have misjudged him , because there was nothing there . Then right before he was about to end the session, he notices that the guy keeps eyeing a set of bleachers ahead of them , one in particular. Pretending to stretch , Ronnie catches the eye of a staff member . Motioning to him using his head and eye's , it isn't long before he gets the hint and starts to look ahead of them into the bleachers , followed by a few others of the staff. With everyone else sitting up and looking ahead with great curiosity , strangely the talkative one now has nothing to say . So odd was it that even one of the younger regulars mentioned it.)

Young patron) " Wow , that's the most dude's been quiet ever since we been in here. "

Mr. Talkative) " I'm just ready ta go home just like everybody else . " (As he looks down to where the staff has reached.)

(Just then , the staff member that Ronnie alerted to search the bleachers calls out)

Staff member) " We found it " (With that he walks the wallet back down to the person that reported it stolen)

(The manager speaking to the patron that brought it to his attention)

Manager) " Is this your wallet ? "

Patron) " Yes "

Manager) " Would you like us to get the police involved ? "

(Hesitating briefly , as he looks at the faces of all the other patrons that voluntarily laid their personal things out on the floor on his behalf , he says)

Patron) " ... No , everything 's here , thank you for your patience . "

Manager) " Alright , ladies and gentleman you can put stuff back in your bags , your free to leave. "

(Then unexpectantly one of the younger patrons has something to say)

Young Patron) " Nah man , hold up . We got a thief up in here , and if y'all thought it was one a us it wouldn't be no happy ending unless somebody was walkin outta here wit they hands behind they back ."

(Oddly , other patrons in the room started to applaud his statement. The manager groans , knowing this has just turned into a long night.)

Manager) " Alright listen , no one's going to jail , nobody's life will be ruined . The only thing that will happen to you is that you will lose your membership here for life. So for the love of God , please come forward so we all can go home. "

(While he's waiting for his words to sink in , another patron makes a statement .)

Patron 2) " That's it ? ... Man I should a stole something tonight ."

Manager) " C'mon now , this is serious , anyone ? "

(With no one coming forward , he calls his staff over and they get in a huddle . While their there , Ronnie notices that the staff member he gave the tip too , keeps looking in his direction . It isn't before long that others are doing it as well. As he thinks to himself for a solution , he knows full well that time is running out , it's very true that he didn't want fanfare , but how can he get around it now. He couldn't tell them how he really found out who the culprit was , so what exactly could he say, it had to be good and it had to be fast , because here they come . The manager scans the room once more , and no one comes forward , now he calls Ronnie over , and they take a few steps away from everyone else .)

Manager) " The staff tells me that you knew where the wallet was , how ? "

(Talking to himself first ," Alright , moment of truth , what cha got ? Truth ? They don't know me , or what I do for a living . " (Now he's prepared to give an answer.)

Ronnie) " I'm a behavioral Scientist , I can read the nonverbal signs that people give off when they have something to hide . I 've worked with the police before on a case .

Manager) " I see ... I'd be forever grateful if you could get to the bottom of this quickly . You see my wife is pregnant and if she doesn't see me home at a certain time she begins to worry and that's bad for her and the baby , so could you please . "

Ronnie) " Of course , no problem . "

Manager) " Can I have your attention please , this is Mr. " (Looking at Ronnie) " Sorry I didn't get your name . "

Ronnie) " Dobbs "

Manager) " Yes , thank you , this is Mr. Dobbs , he works with the police as a behavioral scientist , he was the one that helped us find the wallet and also the one that can tell us who the culprit is , so Mr. Dobbs …"

Ronnie) " Right , thank you , I really hate doing this on the spur of a moment , there's a lot of science involved , but for the sake of time . " (Pointing to Mr. talkative) " There's your man right there ."

Patron 1) " I knew it all along , didn't I tell Y'all , pay the man. (He goes over to three different people and collects)

Manager) " Mr. Thomas ? … You've been coming here for 5 yrs. "

Patron 1) " And probably been stealing the whole time . This ain't the first time uh ah . "

Manager) " Mr. Thomas you are banned from not only this " Power " gym , but all " Power " gyms for life , I need your membership card and your license please . Everyone else , your free to go . Mr. Dobbs , hold on for a minute please. "

Ronnie) (Thinking to himself) " Now you've done it , had to oversell didn't you ? "

MANAGER) " I just wanted to thank you in person for what you did , and to tell you that all your membership fees for the year are taken care of , just come and enjoy yourself . " (Reaches out and shakes his hand.)

Ronnie) " Thank you very much , no problem " (Talking to himself) " Just get out of here man , wow , that was close . " (Now safely in his car he relaxes , then burst out laughing) " Behavioral Scientist , that's a good one I got to remember that , Sophie was right , using this the right way can be a lot of fun. "

(Arriving safely home , he tells Kathryn of all the strange events he encountered on this very strange night. They have a good laugh , enjoy a late dinner then go off to bed . While lying there reviewing his day , he relieves that he hadn't expanded his length of viewing at all , it was still

5 to 7 minutes tops . He would have to take this more seriously . Before drifting off to sleep he remembered a nice park not far from the house . With everyone doing their own thing , he could view them without being detected for as long as he wanted. He smiles to himself , thinking of how simple it was to come up with , and all the benefits he would get out of it. As he begins to drift off to sleep his last thoughts were of Kathryn , and showing her one day how well he mastered his new gift. Morning comes and they go about their regular routine . While at work the only thing he can really stay focused on is the best way to view people at the park . Like a kid waiting for recess at school he continues to watch the clock . Finally it's quitting time , and the race is on. Arriving rather quickly at the park , he reaches in the glove box , gets his shades and off he goes. There's a perfect spot by an old oak tree that has a bench , shade and everything. It sits just off to the side of a track , used for jogging , walking , cycling , roller blading , or just strolling with a little one. Now it's time to choose a subject.)

Ronnie) (Thinking to himself) " Ah yes , a nice thirty something couple . Let's see how long I can hold it " (He locks in and immediately gets disturbed . Still talking to himself .) " Why didn't I think about this before ? I'm not trying to ease drop conversations ; I'm trying to see what they are seeing . The only thing that they will be seeing is the park , not a whole lot of interaction there . (Somewhat dejected) I guess I could go to the mall again ; I don't know. "

(Without realizing it he begins to walk , before long , he's left the park and walking on the sidewalk , when an attractive woman passes by him , snaping him back to his senses.)

Ronnie) " The street , of course . I'm such an idiot . "

(He plops down on a nearby bus bench , and begins to look for subjects .)

Ronnie) (Smiling now , and again he begins thinking to himself) " Since it was a woman that brought me back , let's start there. (Just then a young woman with a small child comes and sits on the bench with him . Still thinking to himself he says) " O.K. universe , we'll start here. "

(He greets the woman , she responds , then they both go about the business of minding their own business . From the greeting he has all he needs to start the viewing , and he does. He sees that she is very attentive to her child , checking her constantly to make sure all is well with her .The loving attention she showers the child with makes him smile . Looking in the opposite direction of her , she has no clue of what was going on . After making sure that the child needs are met , she then takes out her phone ,and instead of making a call , she stars to text. From the text he sees that she is in search of an apartment , and while several pop up with their web pages , she seems to be looking in a certain price range . From the way she keeps wiping her face he could tell that she was getting extremely stressed over the whole situation . No sooner had he realized this that another realization almost made him laugh out loud.)

Ronnie) (Thinking to himself) " She's of Latin descent , so is Oscar , his father owns an apartment complex , you can't make this stuff up . "

(Working at his office for some time , he knows the ins and outs of just about everyone there , and he knows that Connie's always the last to leave , so he whips out his phone and calls the job . Sure enough Connie answers and he ask for Oscar's contact number . In his quest for doing the right thing , what he'd forgotten about Connie was , she was a great person but a stickler for the rules .)

Connie) " Now Ronald you know I can't do that , what, are you trying to get me fired. "

Ronnie) " C'mon Connie you know I wouldn't ask if it wasn't important . "

Connie) " That doesn't help me at all if I'm standing in the unemployment line. "

Ronnie) " Connie , if any of this blow back on you I'll be standing right there in that line with you , and you know I would . "

Connie) " Yes Ronald , I believe you would . Alright , ... wait he's still in the parking lot talking to Amy , those two , hold on let me get him. "

(She does what she said and soon Oscar comes to the phone .)

Oscar) " Hey Mr. Dobbs , Connie said you wanted to speak to me . "

Ronnie) " Yes , do you have your phone with you ? "

Oscar) " Yes sir "

Ronnie) " O.K. listen , I'm going to send you a series of text right now , that I need an answer to right now , O.K. ? "

Oscar) " O.K. Mr. Dobbs , go ahead. "

(Just he begins to send the text , her bus comes , and she and her daughter board it and leaves.)

Ronnie) (Thinking to himself) " Normally this would be the end of a potential good deed , but adding the gift to it changes everything. " (Speaking out loud) " I can talk now , she's gone. "

Oscar) " What's all that noise Mr. Dobbs , I can hardly hear you . "

Ronnie) " It was the bus , doesn't matter, do you still have units available ? "

Oscar) " Yes "

Ronnie) " Good , O.K. , listen you got the information of what she's looking for , correct ? "

Oscar) " Yes ah huh "

Ronnie) " O.K. , now her name is Lucinda Alverez , her cell phone number is (407) 696 -3241 , she's got a small kid and she's kind of desperate right now , so give her a call and get her in , O.K. "

Oscar) " Don't worry Mr. Dobbs , we got her . "

Ronnie) " Thanks Oscar , I owe you one . Put Connie back on ."

Oscar) " Don't' mention it Mr. Dobbs , oh , and Mr. Dobbs , you don't owe me a thing , thank you for Amy , here she goes .... Mr. Dobbs for you. (Hands the phone back to Connie)

Ronnie) " Connie , you had my back, now I'll have yours, Mac loves home cooked meals , you do that and he's yours . "

Connie) " Home cook in huh , I've tried everything but that , thanks Ronald , you are a life saver . "

Ronnie) " So are you Connie , so are you , thanks , bye now "

(He hadn't noticed until that very moment that his viewing time had changed dramatically . He had been viewing her for at least 20 minutes before her bus came . Feeling quite proud of himself with this new accomplishment . He couldn't wait to get home and tell Kathryn all about it ... but this was just the beginning . He hadn't explored enough yet , he wanted to knock her socks off , 20 minutes was good , but how much further could he push it. He began to set weekly goals to increase his limit .Adding 5 minutes a week for the next two weeks , would bring him to 30 full minutes per view . Now he was ready to not only tell Kathryn , but to show her his prowess . The day finally came for his big reveal , and since it was his day off , he decided to take one more test run before she comes home . Being out and about makes him a little thirsty , passing by a smoothie shoppe , he decides to go in , while waiting on his order, he decides to have a quick viewing . At first no one catches his eye , then over in the corner of the shoppe someone does. A Mr. Paul Bryant, at the 30-minute mark where he would usually shut it off , Mr. Bryant's life got really exciting . Being the contractor for a very large office building project. He had gotten himself in trouble about having fake permits for different areas of the job site , and more importantly , the misplacement of $100 thousand dollars was missing from the loan contract. Intrigued , he decides to see a bit more , when something happened. Not only did he see what the subject was seeing , but he also started to hear his thoughts . Frightened by this turn of events , he quickly tries to end the session , but somethings wrong . Just then Kathryn comes home.)

Kat) (frightened she screams) " RONNIE ! " (She runs over to him wanting to shake him , but by now Ronnie has a white glow all around him that gave her pause. Standing nervously near him , she looks around the room for assistance , sees a broom , runs over to retrieve it , runs back and without really thinking , takes a full swing and knocks Ronnie to the floor. As soon as the broom makes contact , the glow vanishes , leaving Ronnie shivering on the floor almost in a fetal position. Quickly recovering after a couple of minutes , he sits up bewildered about the whole affair , and is surprised to see Kathryn .)

Ronnie) " Kat ? ... When did you get home ? "

Kat) " A few minutes ago " (turns away and brush off a tear.)

Ronnie) (concerned) " What happened Kat ? "

Kat) " You were glowing Ronnie , you weren't yourself , and you couldn't hear me. I knocked you on the floor with that broom over there. " (motioning to the broom)

Ronnie) " Glowing ? "

Kat) " if I hadn't come home when I did , I don't know what would have happened." (tear's start to fall , and through them she manages to speak.) " Ronnie , promise me that you won't go back in unless I'm with you . "

Ronnie) (Hesitating , and clearing his throat) " I ... well "

Kat) (shouting) RONNIE ! I'm not coming home finding that you've vanished off the face of the earth , doing something you don't have to do , and don't give me that nonsense about the greater good . Somebody else can do that until you learn what this whole thing is all about , yes ? "

Ronnie) " Yes , " (smiling at her) " When did you become such a fireball ? "

Kat) " When you decided to start glowing . (Thinking for a moment , then asking)" ... Ronnie , you were home when you started to glow , how were you able to see someone at all . ? "

Ronnie) " I went out for a smoothie , and while I was there in the shoppe waiting for my drink nobody really interested me accept this guy . I don't know how to describe it , but it was just something about him , so I started viewing him.

Kat) (confused) " But if you're seeing what he's seeing , how did you get back home ? "

Ronnie) (confused as well) " You know , I don't know ... I locked in on him in the smoothie shoppe and held his image , then I left and came back here . (remembering) I sat down here , (going over t the window seat .) " I pulled him back up , ... (excited) " I pulled him back up ! "

Kat) (still confused) " O.K. , so you thought about him some more ? "

Ronnie) " No ... I hadn't thought about this until now , I pulled him back up ... I could still see what he was seeing ."

Kat) " But ... how is that possible ? "

Ronnie) (Laughing and speaking at the same time) " I don't know , but that's fantastic ! It means we can find out all we need to , without being confined to where we started viewing . " (Seeing her confusion he explains further .) " So let's say I started viewing a woman that interested me " (Seeing her expression change , he changes .) " Scratch that , say I was viewing an old man that was looking at monkeys in the zoo . I could end the session right there , leave the zoo , come home and instead of turning on the T.V. , I could pull him back up , and continue viewing him for as long as I want . "

Kat) " O.K. , let me wrap my head around this , ... you could say be viewing me right here in the house , stop viewing me , go to work , and on your lunch break , you could pull me back up and see what I'm doing ? "

Ronnie) " Yes "

Kat) (Excited and scared at the same time) " Babe that's amazing ... and spooky at the same time . This whole thing is blowing my mind right now ... , let's pull back and let this breathe for a moment ... no , the rest of the day would do just nicely .

Ronnie) " Alright , we'll sleep on it . But I tell you Kat , this guy ... is 10 times worst than the guy at the mall , I have to do something ."

Kat) (seeing his sincerity) " Alright babe , we'll plan it and make sure he pays , but none of that 30-minute business , 20 minutes tops , O.K. ? "

Ronnie) (smiling) " O.K. babe "

(Keeping their word , the rest of the evening and night was uneventful. Allowing them a deep and restful sleep. Next morning they agree to view Mr. Paul Bryant again , just to see what was going on with him . Apparently , the vision of him only last for 24hrs. So a new contact would have to be made . Leaving home an hour earlier would afford Ronnie a chance to see him again , and lend to viewing him 15 to 20 minutes before cutting the session . Sure enough it happens just that way , and the plan works like clockwork . At different points of his day , while in secure places at work , he would peep to see what Mr. Bryant was up to . By the time his day at work was finished , he had the whole layout of what Mr. Bryant's next day would be like. With the both of them safely home , he informs Kathryn of what he's learned , and together they open another session with the broom standing by. The use of a timer is also incorporated . He relays what he sees and she writes it all down , to make an action plan later. The session ends without a hitch , and from the information gathered during the course of the day and evening , they come up with a plan of action .)

Ronnie) " He's meeting Mr. Brunswick at 3 o'clock to get those fake permits , and Miss Clark will be waiting for him at " Northman's " bank at 3:45 , he met with her yesterday for lunch . She's about 5'4 or

5'5 , blonde , small frame , and loves smiling , or maybe that was just for him . "

Kat) " Or the 10 grand he wrote on the sticky you saw . "

Ronnie) (smiling) " Yes that was probably it , (They share a quick laugh , then get back to business) "O.K. as planned , you watch the bank and tell me what happens . I'll stay on him . "

(With assignments given they leave in separate cars to their post , realizing the importance of viewing from a safe distance as not to arouse any type suspicion . On the way to the construction site , he thinks it best to stop off at a local store and pick up a disposable phone , pays cash , and activates it . Knowing all the details of Mr. Byrant's plans , and the players involved , he waits until an hour before the appropriate time ,then makes the call to the police . Half an hour goes by and nothing , not at the office or the bank , 45 minutes go by and still nothing in either spot . Thinking to himself by now that they didn't take his anonymous call seriously , in a risky move he takes out his own phone and is about to call again , fully prepared to give his name and the whole ball of wax . Then a police car shows up , along with an unmarked car , two men in suits get out first and are pointed to Mr. Byrant's office . Just as they reach him , he attempts to run , but to no avail , they quickly catch him throw on the cuffs , and place him in the police car . Just as he's about to call Kathryn with the news , she calls him first and tells pretty much the same story . With mission accomplished they agree to meet each other at one of their favorite restaurants to celebrate .)

Ronnie) " Well , that felt good "

Kat) " And you didn't even have to glow to get it done ."

Ronnie) " That's right ! " (They toast , then Ronnie 's mood turns introspective) " But you do know that there will come a time so severe that I will have to glow to fix it . "

Kat) (smiling) " Still thinking you're a super hero , doing it all on your own . No way buddy , you've got me , and I intend that the only glowing you'll do , is when you see me in that red dress . "

Ronnie) " What red dress ? "

Kat) " You'll see " (They share a laugh , and finish their dining experience . They leave the restaurant perfectly pleased with the outcome of the day . Then start to realize the potential of the gift Ronnie has been given . With all the good coming out of using the gift , they'd forgotten all about the true meaning of the glow until the celebration was truly over . As they readied themselves for bed , Kathryn speaks)

Kat) " You know babe , this glow thing is way over our heads . "

Ronnie) " Yeah, I know (He hesitates momentarily) ... she was right . " (Seeing the confusion on Kathryn's face he continues) " Sophie told me that seers can feel one another , I can tell she's close . We'll track her tomorrow and get to the bottom of all this , O.K. ? "

Kat) (pleased and smiling) " Of course , now let's get some sleep . "

Ronnie) " Sleep ? I thought I thought I was going to see that red dress . "

Kat) (Smiling and almost laughing) " I said " dress " dear not negligee . Besides , I think you've had enough excitement for one day . "

Ronnie) (He makes the movements of a magician) " Now I 've given " you the power " to look into my see's, and tell me what you see . "

(She laughs and comes over to him , he turns out the light and they both giggle in the dark . Next morning as promised he tracks Sophie ; they pin her down to a train station still in Florida . Arriving , they start making their way through the crowd to find her . Much to their surprise , she finds them first

Sophie) " You called ? "

Ronnie) " This is Kathryn my fiancé , she knows everything . "

Sophie) " How do you do , I'm Sophie Monet , (they exchange a pleasant smile)

Kat) " Yes , I've heard of you , Kathryn Slater , " (they politely shake hands) " so nice to meet you."

Sophie) " How may I help you, Ronnie ? "

Ronnie) " I was viewing a person and something happened. "

Sophie) " You mean the glow. (They both looked shocked) " How long were you viewing him ?"

Ronnie) " Over 30 minutes "

Kat) (shocked) " Ronnie ! , Over 30 minutes ? "

Ronnie) " Not much over , I'd say maybe 7 to 8 minutes tops. "

Sophie) " And did you hear his thoughts ? "

Ronnie) " Yes ... how did ? "

Sophie) " Because we've all done it . Myself , and the six others that I told you about ... (Looking at him) now seven . "

Ronnie) " But what was that ? "

Sophie) " It's the tying of two souls , you become a part of them , but you never lose yourself . Think about it this way , you become his or her second conscience . You instruct them to take what you believe to be the right road . You go in to repair their broken conscience . In order to keep that from happening too you , you have from one, to thirty minutes of viewing without an issue , one minute over that, puts you at risk . "

Ronnie) " At risk for what ? "

Sophie) (with a slight devilish grin) " Why becoming them. " (They both stand stunned , then Ronnie finally speaks.)

Ronnie) " I could become them ? For how long ? "

Sophie) " Depends on how involved you are , if you're trying to right a wrong , or change the course of events , depends , could be days...weeks ... until you , say it's done. "

Kat) " If you've done it , how did you get back ? "

Sophie) " Once you've achieved what you think is the proper solution , you let go , after you let go you come back to yourself . "

Kat) " When you say come back , you mean mentally right ? "

Sophie) (smiling) " No , the glow is your energy , your entire being merges with your subject. You're just missing until you decide to come back. "

Ronnie) " I tried to come back , but I couldn't . "

Sophie) " You were in the middle of mind set , seeing the problem , knowing it wasn't right , wanting to fix it , and afraid of what was happening to you , correct ? "

Ronnie) " Is there anymore parts to this thing that I should know. "

Sophie) (Flashing a secretive smile) " I told you when I met you , that there is a whole lot more to this than viewing people . I am sorry that happened to you and you weren't prepared , but you have to be more careful in how you use this . I do apologize , but my time is valuable and I have other places to be today , forgive me. Goodbye my Darling boy " (Looking at Kathryn) " so nice to meet you , goodbye . "

(With that she leaves . As they stand in the middle of the station , not really sure of what to do next , they see a man aimlessly wandering about. Thinking maybe he's drunk or high , they take him lightly , until he says something that catches Ronnie's attention.)

Wandering Man) " I can't see anything , ...what ? "

(Just as Ronnie's about to go over to see if he could assist , an incredible force hurls the man 10 feet , right into the front of an oncoming train . There's an immediate explosion in front of the train where the man was thrown , immediately followed by the squealing from the braking system of the train . Incredibly no one in the crowd , nor on the train was hurt . However , finding any remains of the man could prove to be a challenge . The overwhelming , intense horror of the scene has everyone scurrying for the exits . The entire area of the incident is cleared in a matter of seconds . As the running , screaming crowd leaves the station , Ronnie and Kathryn have little choice but of doing the same . But the thing that kept haunting Ronnie , was the statement the man said before , about not being able to see kept playing over and over in his mind. He remembers vividly that the man seemed surprised of his condition . If he had been blind for some time , there would be no reason for the announcement . After safety returning to their car , the words of the man play one more time . Then like a bolt from the blue he gets it and says)

Ronnie) (low voice at first) " can't be ... (more excited) " Can't be ! "

Kat) (concerned) " Can't be what ?

Ronnie) (staring) " The man on the road... the one I tried to save ; he couldn't see either. That's why he was swerving all over the road until he ran into the tree . Something blinded him , just like this guy. "

Kat) (almost whispering) " You mean he was a seer ? "

Ronnie) " Didn't get a chance to view him , but probably so . "

Kat) " Let's get out of here . "

(As they make their way home each person continues to play all the different scenarios of events they witnessed . Kathryn , ... Ronnie's glowing , and the man at the train station. Ronnie , ...the man on the road where he received his gift , the white bright light , the hearing of Mr. Bryant's thoughts , and the blind man at the station. After sufficiently pondering over the information , they decide mentally to leave it alone . They arrive safely back home without further incident, once inside, feeling num they plop down on the couch . Then a light goes off in Kathryn 's head .)

Kat) " I understand Sophie's smile now . "

Ronnie) " What ? "

Kat) " Sophie , she said there's more to this " (she gasps) " she could be watching us ! Babe , you said it yourself when you first met her , she's had this thing since she was twelve . (Becomes even more shocked) " That means all of you are capable of it . All her six friends and anyone else with the gift , curse , or whatever this is ... it makes all of you a higher-level peeping Tom or Tomacina . "

Ronnie) " Wow , that's a lot ... of course everything you said is true , but the difference would be , who gave us this power . I heard it somewhere , I can't remember where , but we are carefully chosen for this. Only people with a certain character are given the gift . Because whoever bestows it upon us knows we're not going to abuse it . "

Kat) " Remember the man in the car , he didn't have time to approve you , he was dying , so he just passed it along . " (Hearing this makes Ronnie smile , puzzling Kathryn)

Ronnie) " So that's what he meant . I 've been trying to figure that out ever since that night . "

Kat) " Figure out what , and why are you smiling ? "

Ronnie) " He said , " Thank God " then gave me the gift , and threw me far enough out of the way that I wouldn't be hurt. It all makes sense now , I was chosen . Be it by some random selection by nature , or by divine decree . We have a code and we have power. It's like she said , there's more to this than just viewing people . "

(All the revelations of the day and everything they witnessed leave them speechless. They sit in silence allowing their brains to catch up . They both decide after a while to leave it alone , and are just settling in when there's a knock at the door. Somewhat puzzled , Ronnie answers.)

Ronnie) " Who's there ? "

Sophie) " It's me dear boy . "

Ronnie) (Quickly opening the door) " Sophie ? ... What's going on ? "

Sophie) (A little shaken) " I should have told you then , ... but I could feel they were close . "

Kat) " Who ? "

Sophie) (a little hesitant) " ... The Others "

Ronnie) " What others ? What do you mean ? "

Sophie) " Do you have something strong here ? Whiskey , Burbon , anything ? "

Kat) " Just some wine from Christmas. "

Sophie) " That will do. " (They give her the wine , stand close, and wait impatiently for an explanation , after a couple of gulps, she begins.) " Can we all sit down please , and I'll tell you everything ."

(They quickly agree and motion's her to the dinner table . She takes one more gulp , steady's herself , and begins.)

Sophie) " The man at the station name was Roger Parks , a dear friend of mine. We would go on holiday together whenever I was in the states. We were in the process of planning another holiday , when you arrived . I knew my conversation with you wouldn't take that long , and I'd return to continue our planning . While planning , Roger and I would play a harmless game of guessing what someone might be seeing before we viewed them , we would make little wagers along the way, to make it interesting . He was always better at it than I ,and would win most of the time , he had a natural knack . He'd chosen someone else to start a new match with , but I told him I'd be coming out to speak with you , so he decided he'd do a regular viewing until I returned . After speaking with you on my way back to him , the person he decided to view was being used by " the others " , no sooner had he started to view them" the others " intercepted the viewing , causing him to go blind , ... the rest you know . In all the commotion , leaving seemed the best option , so I did ."The Others " are not like us , they prey on non seer's , getting them to blame one another for the acts of violence that they lead them to commit , while they hang back in the shadows . We only learned about them a few years ago , when we started being attacked . We knew that they could detect a seer's presence if they stayed in too long. But we had no idea that they could detect our presence less than the 30 minutes rule .

Kat) " How do they do that ? "

Sophie) " They take control of the signal , and blind the host , not being able to see anything , the host and the seer are at the mercy of " the other . "

Ronnie) " But they only killed Mr. Parks , not the host. "

Sophie) " Yes, this was new , we had no idea they could do that. Which makes them extremely dangerous ."

Ronnie) " So before today , if a seer was viewing someone for longer than 30 minutes , and "the other " intercepted the signal , could the seer pull out ? "

Sophie) " No , once attached their energy starts to merge , giving " the other " complete control.

Ronnie) " So the seer never comes back ? "

Sophie) " Never " (reaching out putting a hand on both of them) " Before this new business with " the others " started . As I mentioned before I started to glow , but I didn't understand it the same as you , there I was sucked into someone else's brain not really knowing how to get out . But my youth saved me. Hearing his thoughts and remembering what my dear Aunt taught me about right and wrong , I was able to maneuver him to making the right choice , just as soon as he did what I led him to do , I felt a warm rush of complete joy come over me , and in an instant , I was back . Still wearing the same clothes that I was wearing when I left. But that was five days earlier . I've done it a few times since then , not always with the same happy outcome . When they flat out refuse to do what you think is right , that's when you separate , you let go , come back to yourself , and leave them to their own devices . I tell you this to show you how deep this goes . I've been married 5 times , and have lost them all , partly for their sakes , partly for mine . The one's I really cared about I had to let them go. Plugging into someone else's life and assisting them in making the right choices , and making sure that they are caught if they do not , is very hard on relationships. Disappearing totally sometimes for weeks on end , will put a death nail to a marriage. The ones I didn't care all that much about I let them leave me. Learning from all this , at least for me , that it's better not to become too attached to anything or anyone . Being wealthy has been a great comfort to me , until " the other's " started showing themselves ."

Kat) " Just how many are there ? "

Sophie) " I don't know , but I would imagine , like us they are everywhere. "

Ronnie) " I realize that you didn't know that they could do what they did today but , question.... why didn't you just stop viewing beyond 30 minutes , then no one would have been able to track you , you would be safe , and could stop all the running ... I imagine that's why you travel so much and have little time to spend with anyone. You expect that " the others " would find you , I'm I right ? "

Sophie) " Of course your right dear boy , but we've been entrusted with this gift for a reason . I've done what you've suggested from time to time, but I always end up feeling ashamed . "

Ronnie) " Has anyone ever killed one of them ? "

Kat) (shocked) " Ronnie ! "

Ronnie) " If it comes down killing them to keep you safe , you know my vote. "

Sophie) " No Ronnie , I've never heard of anyone killing them. "

Ronnie) " Everything has a balance , we can only go so far before we're hurt , the same thing has to apply to them. Call a meeting for everyone you know , and instruct all them to do the same . With all of us working on this problem together , there has to be a solution . "

Sophie) " My darling boy , O.K. I'll do it "

(Within a week forty seers from all over the country and abroad converge on a little spot Sophie put together from her travels. Knowing the looming threat , they all wait impatiently for a solution.)

Wendel from Georgia) " I've been sitting here for a while now , and ain't nobody said nonthin bout fix in this. I been attacked , just like other people I know , and it's only been the good lord that made it somebody that they were controlling , attack in us stead a them. "

Beaver from Wichita Kansas) " Seems ta me that these attacks are an affront to everything we stand for , so um open for any suggestions that the group might have ta fight back as it were. "

Bob from Denver) " We live , we die , we do it all together , so why is this any different , we fight these things wherever we find them . I say we find out what their weakness is and give it too um good . "

Amy from Scottsdale Arizona) " I for one am tired of being pushed around by these things , it's time we showed them what it's like to be afraid . "

(Testimonies ring out from the unfortunate ones that had run-ins with " the others " before.)

Betsy from Tennessee) " My John was taken from me when one of those " others " made him so depressed about his job situation that it made him kill four other innocent people before of course he was dealt with by the troopers . But we all knew that it wasn't him , that man would feel bad about squashin a bug , let alone a human being ."

Harper from Australia) " Good day , I'm not in the habit of makin speeches but my Jack and I had a run in with one these things , he got in the head of Mary (starts to cry) six she was , got a hold of his bush knife and carved him up good before I could stop her. Sweet as molasses she is , loves her dad , the two of them are tighter than the queen's stockings . She would've never hurt her dad were it not for them. "

Wade from Texas) " Well , I kind a hate to follow that , cause compared to that well , mine's not that bad. Anyhow , one at these things got a hold of my Cheryl , that's my wife. I got home from work came into the kitchen like I always do , and knew somethin was wrong , the room had a smokey grey looking tint to it ,and a little bit of grey smoke was coming out of her . She was just sittin there starin at nothin . So soon as I went over and shook her , the room got light again , the staring stopped and the grey smoke vanished. She woke up wantin ta know what happened . I shutter ta think what would a happened if I didn't come home on time . "

(As testimonies dwindle , the overwhelming consensus is that someone has to lead the attack .)

Sophie) " I've , we've heard all your concerns . But this meeting is about solutions. "

Liam from Canada) " I say we study them , the same as they must have studied us . A small test group put in motion that reports what they find back to the rest of us , should give us at least a good starting point . "

Sophie) " And just who do you have in mind for such a task ? "

Liam) " The three of you called this thing, and you have my backing to see it through . "

Sophie) (Looking around the room) " Anyone else with something to say ? "

George from England) " It seems that from all accounts we've heard mentioned today , that for whatever reason " the others " are only interested in America . "

Kat) " Please tell me you just didn't say that , it's an American problem ? "

George) " My meaning is to say , that we all will be very supportive in your endeavor , but Americans should lead the way. "

(From the rumblings around the room , the majority seem to agree with this new way of thinking. With there being no push back to making it a united front Ronnie stands up)

Ronnie) " Alright ! ... I'll do it ." (Incredibly shocked by this , Kathryn jumps up as well.)

Kat) " Ronald No ! ... no , there has to be a better way. (Angrily viewing the crowd) " He's still new to all of this ! Is there anyone here fresher than he ! But you would sit there in silence and allow him to risk his life for the good of all of you. " (Now Sophie stands up)

Sophie) " Kathryn 's right , all of us have had the gift for a while some of us, for a long time. We owe it ourselves and to the one's that entrusted us with this gift to preserve whatever good is left in the world and fight for it ... so , I will be with him as well ... is there anyone else. "

(After some murmuring back and forth it stills comes down to Sophie , her five friends, Ronnie and Kathryn . At the meeting's conclusion , Kathryn is noticeably disturbed .)

Kat) " Well this was a complete waste of time. "

Sophie) " Not really , now we have actual contact information on other seers that we did not have before. "

Kat) " Please don't use that word. "

Sophie) " What word ? "

Kat) " Others " (Looking in Ronnie's direction) " you've been strangely quiet , after you thru your own self under the bus ."

Ronnie) " I'm sorry , but after hearing everyone's tales about " the others" , just has me working things out in my head. "

Kat) (speaking in a soft tone) " I hate when he does this . "

Sophie) " Why ? "

Kat) " Because he always figures it out , and this is the one time I hope he doesn't.

Ronnie) (Thinking out loud) " Wade from Texas said , that when his wife got influenced by one, that the room had a smoky gray tint to it , and just shaking her brought her back ."

Sophie) " But she wasn't a seer , she was just someone about to be used to do something.

Ronnie) " But he could see that. " The other " , was in essence doing what we do , see through someone else' s eyes . What if the same thing applies to them , if they stay in too long , will they also be trapped."

(As the two women begin to process what was being said to them , he continues.)

Ronnie) " In the case of the guy going all over the road when I got this thing. To Roger Parks at the train station . "The other '" was in and out in less than 30 minutes ... I think I'm right , whether on a normal person or a seer , the same rule applies , everybody has a 30-minute window.

Kat) " But even if that's true , in the case of Mr. Parks , he died. "

Ronnie) " Yes , but that was because only one seer was connected , but what about two, seeing the same person. "

Sophie) " Could work , but once you trap him , how do you get rid of him without killing the host ?"

Ronnie) " Haven't thought that far yet , But I'm working on it. "

Kat) (inquisitive) " Sophie , you said at the train station you knew they were close , how ? "

Sophie) " I've had the gift since I was twelve , so I automatically sense danger when my surroundings start to change. "

Kat) " Like what ? "

Sophie) " Well , ... things start to get lightly grey , smoke like , then a sense of foreboding . Heeding these feelings have probably saved my life countless times. "

Ronnie) " Good , we can definitely use that " (He starts to mentally process information , after a minute or two his facial expression changes) " OH "

Kat) " What ? "

Ronnie) " For this to work , we will have to take some time off from work for a while . "

Sophie) " No ... not for a while , you do not work anymore , we're partners now . Anything that you need I will supply . " (They look at her in surprise) " Don't be too surprised my beautiful darlings , we can't have you work and fight a war at the same time now, can we ? I've been rich since I was 12yrs old. Since that time , I've doubled what was given to me , then doubled it again. I've been wealthy for quite some time now , and what I am saying by saying all of that is that , I will fund everything we need to get the job done , period. Upon the conclusion of this war , I will also make both you rich as well. "

Kat) " If we live long enough . " (They all share a smile .)

Ronnie) " Right , ... (looking at Sophie) you're five other friends , can we count on them ? "

Sophie) " Of course "

Ronnie) " Good , we'll need them to help set the trap. " (looking at Sophie) " you said that you can sense them , right ? "

Sophie) " YES "

Ronnie) " So we'll use the internet to focus on areas they might be operating in. Places where things suddenly go bad, like unusual disasters or crime spikes that are over the top. I say we start right here in Florida first, then branch out.

Kat) " O.K. man with the plan , so what's next after we find the area ? "

Ronnie) " We make sure we have the best communications that money can buy , and world class watch's with up to the second timers . We would all have to be mic 'd up for the safety of the group , to stay in constant contact. We go to an area with the grey smoke and pick a person, any person , and start to view them . We seem to be cat nip to " the others " , so no matter who they are viewing , they'll pull off of them just to chase us. Once they do ... hopefully, they view like we do , one seer at a time. We then use the contact with each other to take him out .

Kat) " Babe , I'm sure you've thought this through in your own head. But I think you kind a left us in the dark about certain parts of the plan. "

Ronnie) (understanding) " Right , yes um sorry , O.K. , all of us reach the designated spot and spread out to an area where we can have constant visual on one another . Then we watch everyone else. When we see the grey like smoke , one of us will pick a person to view , " the other " will sense a seer's presence . While he is trying to pin point the seer , we'll be pin pointing him. It's said that a seer couldn't view one another , but no one said that a seer couldn't view one of "the others " .

Once " the other " is identified one of us will lock in and start viewing him . If my logic is correct , viewing him will make him see nothing but light , blinding him or her with that wonderful brilliant white light , huh ? Well what do you think ? "

Sophie) " My darling boy , my brilliant clever boy , I think it will work ! "

(They all start to celebrate the plan , but after a minute or two , Kathryn stops celebrating . Noticing , Ronnie asks)

Ronnie) " what's wrong ? "

Kat) " The train station "

Ronnie) " What about it ? "

Kat) " He threw Roger Parks 10 feet right into the train. We don't have that kind of power , do we ?

Sophie) " No ... but if ... (thinking to herself , then a warm smile comes over her face .)

Ronnie) " What ? "

Sophie) " We continue , once we have him in the brightness , all of us continue viewing him . All that brightness will do its own damage , it's impossible to hurt someone when you can't see anything . "

(Now they truly celebrate , and share the plan with the rest of the team. They agree to take the night off to enjoy themselves , before going into battle . Next morning Sophie makes some calls , by noon , the equipment and the instructors versed in it start to arrive . Everyone ' s versed on the communications gear , and make sure that all the timers are working properly on the watches . Other things also start to arrive that were not discussed .

Kat) " What are these ? "

Sophie) " The latest in stun technology . "

Ronnie) " Stun guns ? "

Sophie) " Would you prefer the real ones ; I can just make a call. "

Ronnie) " No , no , stun guns will do just fine ... never know what can happen , ... so what are these ? "

Sophie) " Locator's , good for 24hrs. or until you past them .

Ronnie) " What , you swallow these ? "

Sophie) " Yes , I've used all of this before , for different reasons of course . But it will keep you safe , until we know what we're dealing with , better safe than sorry. "

Ronnie) " I agree , alright everyone , let's get loaded up and start checking possibilities ."

(Within a few minutes they have several hits, most in Florida , two in New York , and one in Mississippi , they decide on a spot close to them in Florida , a bus terminal . After a quick check of their equipment , they decide to also swallow the locators and take the stun guns . Ready for whatever problems come their way , confidently they enter the terminal . Spreading out with visuals on one another as per plan , they communicate back and forth seeking the best area. Soon , they're in the perfect spot and Ronnie is the first in , he picks a middle-aged woman with a pull luggage rack that's loaded with different assortments of colored bags . She looks minorly interesting at first, until he notices that there's a faint grayish smoke coming from her . At first, he thought he was being paranoid , and she was just smoking , but looking at both hands he saw no cigarette . Just to be sure he moves a bit to the right to see if it was in her mouth , it was not. After alerting the team , he decides to view her , he's only in 5 minutes when his vision starts to flicker.)

Ronnie) (Broadcasting in a low tone but very nervous.) " Somebody's trying to get a lock on me , everybody scan your areas , quickly. "

(Three members of the group have nothing to report, a fourth is mistaken . As precious seconds tick away, Ronnie gets extremely nervous now.)

Ronnie) (still whispering) " C'mon guys , the lights are starting to go out ! "

(Just then , Sophie answers)

Sophie) " I have him ! Thin man in red Polo shirt , dark trousers . "

(With that she immediately locks onto him. Within seconds he grabs his head with both hands . Then two more members of the team lock on as well. All the extra power gives him extreme pain and soon he cries out.)

Other) " MY HEAD , TOO MUCH LIGHT ! I CAN'T SEE , I CAN'T SEE !!! "

(With that his head explodes , shortly after, his body does as well , leaving a dark tar like substance scattered 10 feet in every direction . With mission accomplished they all just turn away and move along with the frightened crowd . Losing sight of Ronnie , Kathryn turns back into the crowd and weaves her way back to find him. Remembering that she's mic'd up she calls out to him.)

Kat) " Ronnie , Ronnie respond , (getting concerned) I need you to talk to me babe , Ronnie ! " (Listening closely she believes she hears something .) " say again babe , say again ! " (She stops and turns her head from side to side , listening . Then calls out to him once more.) " Ronnie ! "

Ronnie) (Weakened) " I'm here Kat , "

(She turns slightly and sees him. Quickly making her way to him , she swallows him up in her arms , kiss's him and helps him leave the building . By now the rest of the team have made their way back to the vehicles awaiting Kathryn and Ronnie's return. Just before they start to wonder, Ronnie and Kathryn appear. Seeing she's in need of assistance , two members of the team go out to help them. With everyone safely back now , they assess themselves.)

Sophie) " My darling boy , are you alright ? "

Ronnie) " A little weak , but yeah, I'm fine . "

Kat) (concerned) " Can you see me baby , can you see me? "

Ronnie) (Looking at her and smiling) " Never seen anything so beautiful in all my life. " (They kiss and the whole team erupts in celebration. Satisfied , now they discuss the mission.)

Team member 1) " Did you see that ? His whole head exploded ; it was great ! "

Team member 2) " Think we've got something here ! "

Ronnie) " Thank all of you for acting so quickly. "

Kat) " It was Sophie that locked on him first. "

Ronnie) (Looking at Sophie) " My darling girl . " (He extends his arms and gives her a big hug.)

Sophie) " You're going to make me blush . " (She smiles warmly for a bit , then snaps back into business mode.) " Everyone get on your phones and call all your contacts . Let them know what happened here , and how they can use the same tactic . We'll drive these " others " back to where ever they came from. "

(They all celebrate momentarily , then start making calls. By next morning , calls start pouring in from all parts of the country and beyond , congratulating them for the first victory over " the others . " In return all were given the exact model of how to copy their success . Victories quickly pile up all over the country, and now it's " the others " that are losing ground . Fewer incidents of sudden chaos are being reported now . Staying true to the deadly information that they received , no seer has fallen in months . At this point the original crew decides to take some time off to recharge . Ronnie , Kathryn , and Sophie are inseparable now , and agree to spend their time off together . After a time of relaxing , and enjoying all life's treasure's , they all agree that returning to a more structured life would be best. As they spend their last night of leisure together , Ronnie asks Sophie a very interesting question.

Ronnie) " Is there always an explosion when the gift is exchanged and the giver passes on ? "

Sophie) " It happened calmly with me , no explosion , no real fanfare at all , just the bright brilliant white light in my case ... why do you ask ? "

Ronnie) " The train station , the man on the road with me. Both cases followed with an explosion . "

Kat) " What are you getting at babe ? "

Ronnie) " I feel like we're missing something . "

Sophie) " Like what ? "

Ronnie) " From what I've seen when we die , there's a white light . When they die a black tar like thing. It's gnawing at me , I'll get it ... also , the power they possess .

Sophie) " You mean , throwing Roger into an oncoming train ."

Ronnie) " Yes exactly ! Why don't we have that ? If we're two sides of the same coin and all ."

Sophie) " You might have something there , hang on . Let me make some calls and see what I come up with. "

Kat) (Shaking her head at Ronnie in disapproval) " Couldn't leave well enough alone, could you ? We're winning , isn't that enough ? "

Ronnie) " It would be if it ended there , but it won't . You know it and I know it . There's going to be a push back at some point , and we have to ready for it. If we have untapped power, we need to know about it , why are you upset ? "

Kat) " Remember the first plan ? Who was the first one in ? You were Ronnie , if this gets worse, how am I to know if you won't be the first one in again ! "

(As she gets up to leave , tears start to fall. In full stride she passes Sophie who is on her way back with news. Noticing Kathryn passing in tears , she blows out some air , and returns to Ronnie. She gazes at him without saying a word , he gets the message.)

Ronnie) " She's concerned about me taking risks . (She just stands there glaring at him) " Yes, I know I'll fix it , ... I'm going right now . "

(He goes into their room where she's lying across the bed . Touching her softly on her leg)

Ronnie) " I got it babe , listen , I'll come up with the plan and let someone else take the lead this time , O.K. ? "

(She rolls over and reaches for him . He goes over to where she is , they hug , then gives her a kiss , and decides to stay with her . Concerned , Sophie approaches their door , just as she's about to knock , she sees the light under the door go out. Smiling to herself , she quietly moves away. Next morning at breakfast , after some small talk , Sophie starts to discuss the information she received the night before .)

Sophie) '" We all see the light , that's how we receive our gift , explosions seem to happen only when we are trying to protect . "

Ronnie) " Protect what ? "

Sophie) " Those receiving the gift and those that might get hurt when the power can't be transferred . In Roger's case , there was no one there for him to entrust with the gift .So he made sure no one would be hurt because of it. "

Ronnie) " He threw his self in front of that train ? Why would he do that? "

Sophie) (somberly) " He did it for me . "

Kat) " How , he couldn't even see you ? "

Sophie) " He knew I was there , and I would try to save him . Doing what he did would satisfy "the other " and he would not be interested in harming anyone else. " (Seeing the pain in her face , they show compassion by giving her a hug . With the moment passing Ronnie has a thought .)

Ronnie) " So ... we do have power , but we only use it in protection . Then that means they'll only use there's for destruction , 10 feet in every direction. Is the tar like stuff harmful ?"

Sophie) " I don't know , I'll have to ask ."

Kat) " What are you thinking ? "

Ronnie) " They die as they 've lived , destroying and hurting people . "

Sophie) " I'll make some calls . "

(With that she leaves , while Kat and Ronnie discuss other minor topics of what they've learned over a period of time , she returns .)

Sophie) " The black stuff burns lava hot for only a few seconds if it doesn't land on a human , if it does , it burns down to the bone. "

(Stunned by this new revelation , they sit in silence for a bit , then Ronnie is first to speak .)

Ronnie) " We have to reach more of them at one time. "

Kat) " How ? "

Sophie) " We sponsor an event . "

Ronnie) (catching the thought) " I see where you're going with this , ... it has to be over the top big ! Something that no " other " worth his salt would miss ...but what ? "

Kat) (smiling) " Not one event , but several , all over the country. All happening at the same time , on the same day. A huge event , where all dark secrets will be exposed to the light. "(Now Ronnie catches the vision)

Ronnie) " No more secrets , no more lies , just the truth . "

Sophie) " To be held in places where huge audiences can fit into , and to be simulcasted on huge screens . "

Kat) " Great ! ... now what do we say ? "

Sophie) " All the leaders of this secret fight will be there to ask for your support . "

Ronnie) " But , how do we separate " the others " from the regular humans ? "

Kat) " A light screening , we know " the others " hate white light , it blinds them . If we use a white light scanner , "

Ronnie) " It should give them a headache . Embarrassed , we apologize profusely and gift them with a special VIP pass with our compliments . "

Sophie) " Not only that , we supply them with special 3D shades , that allows them to view the whole event up close and personal. "

Kat) " In the privacy of their own VIP lounge . "

Ronnie) " Automatic locks that we control . Once inside , there's no escape . "

Sophie) " We start the show , turn on the white lights in all the VIP areas , and let the explosions begin. "

Kat) " And with the real show we'll do as promise , and expose these dark figures to the light.

Sophie) " Of course you do understand we will not get them all . "

Ronnie) " I know , but all the ones we do get will put a big dent in their numbers , and once the public knows about them , we stan to have even better odds. "

Sophie) " My darling boy and his incredible girl , I love it ! This event will require the highest level of secrecy and I don't feel that comfort level with anyone else but the team . All other teams and anyone else that we'll need for the set up of the event , will be on a need-to-know basis . "

Kat) " But how can we pull off something this massive without full disclosure ? "

Sophie) " Being wealthy affords me many contacts, and many things at my disposal . I can get all this set up in record time , without full disclosure , give me 3 weeks. "(She walks away smiling with phone in hand making calls .)

(Being true to her word, Sophie does indeed set the date of the big event in the allotted time . With her team in full control, all details are agreed on by them alone . All areas that will house " the others " are meticulously checked and rechecked for optimum efficiency . All printed materials that will be used on that day are drawn up by them , and would only be printed on that day , while all " the others " are safely tucked away in their V.I.P. suites . All equipment and anything else needed for the cleanup will be kept close by , but well out of sight . With plan in place throughout the country , a date is set for the airing of the big event. The networks do their job in promoting as well as the internet and cellular service . Having all participants versed in their rolls , everyone eagerly awaits the big day. The team sends out its final checks and assignments , finally the big day comes. The atmosphere is electric , as hundreds of thousands of people are pigeon into their particular areas to await the big news. Meanwhile, "the others " unknowingly are playing their role , as they are removed from an unsuspecting public . Alone in their VIP lounges they salivate for the moment that they can take charge of the event; all they require is a live feed . Looking into the eyes of the presenters, they will be able to take them out. Putting in one last precaution to hold them in place , the team decides to put in a prerecorded announcement. Telling " the others " that the creators of the program will visit them via internet , and will speak to them directly , and will also give them first peek of the information that will be exposed. They're further told that the 3D shades they were given with their VIP passes will bring them almost eye to eye with the presenters. Having the best of the best proves to be a good selling point to keep "the others " in their place . As they mingle around , drinking from several exotic flowing fountains , while eating rich delicacies blissfully unaware that there are no servers present . The music starts and another prerecorded message tells " the others " that now is the time to put on their 3D shades . What is not mentioned to them is that their special 3D shades are designed to allow all light into their eyes. As soon as the music stops , all doors housing " the others " are automatically locked. Now all of the large screens all across the country are linked into the VIP lounges . For a brief moment there is two – way viewing , and the arrogant " others " start to celebrate their good fortune of being VIP's as they toast the screens with food and drink in their hands. Then , on command , in a flash , all the white lights in their swank VIP lounges are turned on , and the horror show begins. The explosions , painful crying and cursing , vengeful yelling and screams full of terror, are heard and witnessed , at that exact moment Ronnie appears on stage.)

Ronnie) " Ladies and gentleman what you are witnessing on the big screen is real." (Sophie comes out)

Sophie) " This is not a joke , hoax , or any such thing. " (Kathryn comes out)

Kat) " This is the secret fight we've had with these creatures for some time.

(The shocked audience view the large screens in almost utter silence . Soberly the entire nation watches as hundreds of " the other 's " explode right before their eyes . As Ronnie begins again)

Ronnie) " These creatures wish harm to all of us , they work in the shadows , causing chaos among us , making us blame ourselves for everything wrong in the world. When it is they that wish to rule over us. "

(Soon the silence turns to applause , and the applause to cheers , as they witness " the others " meet their doom .)

Kat) " The plan was to hurt them badly today . But , as good as this looks , we couldn't have erased them all. So we are asking you to stay vigilant and use what you see here today to eradicate them . "

Sophie) " We have prepared special literature released today that further explains what we are saying to you now. "

Ronnie) " So please don't be afraid to join the fight. "

(With that said they all pause and watch the screens until the last of " the others " are destroyed . Enlightened and informed the countless crowds cheer and applaud the heroes of the show , then disperse in orderly fashion . Clean up crews arrive armed with intense light weapons , and brilliant light systems on their heavy equipment . On command , all doors are unlocked and swung opened , and the heavy equipment moves in scooping up what's left of "the others " , a huge black tar like mess , mixed with singed body parts are everywhere , making clean -up a massive undertaking . A mission driven dedicated crew moves in somberly, realizing the immense damage these hundreds of bodies could have inflicted on the human race , they feel very fortunate being on this side of the battle . Knowing full well that this could have been them if " the others " were given the chance. This was a sight not meant for the faint of heart , and only the bold need apply . This one particular victory would deeply wound " the others " and would signal the end of any dominance they had in America , along with the secrecy in which they operated under . Now , with a new enemy to focus on , the entire country is energized , armed with the information given them , everyday Joe's are doing incredible things as they take on "the others " wherever they find them . At long last we are finally the " United States " of America . Rightfully , Sophie , Ronnie and Kathryn are recognized as National Hero's , and are given all the honor due them . However , after an all too brief period politics takes over , and before long , it's business as usual . As greedy men push their own agender in the conflict , by now Kathryn , Ronnie and Sophie are no longer needed at the forefront , and they decide to retire from the fight . Meanwhile ,keeping true to her promise , Sophie make's Ronnie and Kathryn very rich indeed , and they now have a very spacious , very beautiful mansion to call home . Parked out front of it ,are two twin BMW X5's , and a bank account that keeps them smiling all the day long , all of which makes them quite comfortable in their new surroundings . As they all spend their final night together before saying goodbye to Sophie with the coming of a new day , they reminisce over all the adventures shared , leaving a sense of nostalgia over the room before they turn in for the night . The following day after a late breakfast and an early lunch , it's time for Sophie to leave. Laughing all through her quick packing , the trio continue to recall all the funny stories that have made their quest more bearable . With the packing done , they make their way through to the rear of the large house, to a beautifully decorated patio that leads to a white dock, that leads down to a lake where a sea plane is waiting. As they all stand on the porch awkwardly , Sophie finally speaks .)

Sophie) " Well my darling boy and my brilliant girl , feel free to call me anytime , and we'll spend some time together. "

(They exchange hugs and kisses , and she leaves them . While they continue watching her from the patio she turns slightly and waves again , they return the wave , and continue holding one another in a half hug . They watch until she boards the plane , just before the pilot closes the door, she scoots up to get one more look at them , smiling , she sits back , and the plane restarts its engines and begins to taxi down the lake . Smiling , the couple watch's the plane until it's in the air , then turn to go back inside. Once inside, they both plop down on the couch , then a listless expression comes over both their face's. Kathryn's first to speak.)

Kat) " So... this is what it feels like to be rich , huh ? Having absolutely nothing worthwhile to do."

Ronnie) " Yeah ... really great huh ? "

(Then, simultaneously they look at each other and Ronnie's the first to speak)

Ronnie) " I hear Europe is struggling with their " other " problem . " (She lovingly looks at him and smiles)

Kat) " She left her number ; we can call her back ! "

(Just then they hear a plane flying low , looking at each other and smiling they run to the patio. As they arrive , they see Sophie's plane circling , coming in for a landing. With childlike exuberance , and widen smile they stand gazing in total disbelief .)

Ronnie) " How did she ? "

Kat) " Who cares, let's go ! "

(Running quickly back inside , they feverishly start grabbing things they might need as well as some things they don't . Accessing one another as they scurry about , they suddenly stop and bust out laughing at each other's break neck pace . By the time they gather a few things and make their way to the dock, Sophie flings the door open , with a huge smile she say's)

Sophie) " You called ? "

(Laughing at her response they board the plane , as they do, she kisses each one . Seeing the amazement on their faces on how she seems to always know what they are thinking , she simply says)

Sophie) " We're family now , of course I want you were I am. "

(With them safely seated, the plane begins its taxi over the lake . When Ronnie suddenly remembers something , causing him to take a deep sigh.)

Kat) " What's the matter babe ? "

Ronnie) " My fault , ... in all the excitement I forgot to lock up . "

Sophie) " Relax my darling boy , I already called. A team is coming in to clean , lock and store your home for you until you return , you never have to worry about anything anymore , my darling boy and my brilliant girl , you're with me now. "

Ronnie) (smiling) " Now that things have slowed down a bit, there is something I always wanted to ask you from the moment I met you , ... why do you call me that ? "

Sophie) " Call you what ? "

Ronnie) " My darling boy "

Sophie) " Because it suits you , would you prefer that I stop saying it. "

Ronnie) (smiling) " No , I think I'd miss it .

(As they take to the air the women start their chatter , leaving Ronnie to relive all the different points of his life that these two women are now a part . Smiling at them both , he remembers past experiences , knowing far too well that it's not even close to being over , pondering the thought further, he finally brings himself to a workable solution as he recites this mantra to himself.)

Ronnie) " You may not see me , but I see you , just remember , someone is always watching. "

The End

Don't miss out!

Visit the website below and you can sign up to receive emails whenever Nathan E publishes a new book. There's no charge and no obligation.

https://books2read.com/r/B-A-DBEDB-EFHDD

BOOKS 2 READ

Connecting independent readers to independent writers.

Did you love *Seeing Things (Full version)*? Then you should read *The Glitz*[1] by Nathan E!

Story of a elderly black woman who runs into something not of this world , angel ,demon,or alien, who really knows ,and how does this all connect to her.

Read more at nephriam@yahoo.com.

---

1. https://books2read.com/u/bQpzqP

2. https://books2read.com/u/bQpzqP

Also by Nathan E

Grandfather Clock
The Squirrel
The Glitz
Seeing Things
Seeing Things (Full version)

Watch for more at nephriam@yahoo.com.

About the Author

A free thinker that loves a good story.
Read more at nephriam@yahoo.com.